MW00906544

THE HURDY-GURDY MAN

by

MARGERY WILLIAMS BIANCO

Illustrated by

ROBERT LAWSON

WITH A NEW INTRODUCTION BY
MARY M. BURNS

GREGG PRESS
BOSTON

With the exception of the Introduction, this is a complete
photographic reprint of a work first published in New York by
Oxford University Press New York in 1933.

The trim size of the original hardcover edition was 7 by 7¼
inches.

Text copyright, 1933, by Oxford University Press New York,
Inc.

Reprinted by arrangement with Jean W. Bianco

Introduction copyright © 1980 by Mary M. Burns

New material designed by Barbara Anderson

Gregg Press Children's Literature Series logo by
Trina Schart Hyman.

Printed on permanent/durable acid-free paper and bound in
the United States of America.

Republished in 1979 by Gregg Press, A Division of G.K. Hall &
Co.,
70 Lincoln St., Boston, Massachusetts 02111

First Printing, January 1980

Library of Congress Cataloging in Publication Data

Bianco, Margery Williams, 1880-1944.
  The hurdy-gurdy man.

  (Gregg Press children's literature series)
  Reprint of the ed. published by Oxford University Press, London.
  SUMMARY: The hurdy-gurdy man's melodies have a dramatic
effect on the stodgy inhabitants of a neat and prosperous little village.
  [1. Music—Fiction.] I. Lawson, Robert, 1892-
1957. II. Title. III. Series.
PZ7.B4713Hu 1979   [E]   79-18020
ISBN 0-8398-2603-6

Introduction

ATTEMPTING to predict which of the books published for children in any given year will become classics is likely to be a demonstration of bravado rather than infallibility. For books, like other art forms, reflect and reaffirm the social and cultural climate in which they were produced. With rare exceptions, they are, like hemlines, subject to the whims of fashion. Only in retrospect can a more informed attempt be made to winnow the timeless from the merely timely; the innately significant from the historical curiosities.

The difference between contemporary recognition and a later-day reassessment may be perceived as one way of distinguishing reviewing from criticism. The former is, after all, a view of the prospect; the other, a view in perspective, for, as Paul Heins so ably stated:

Reviewers do not sift for eternity; they are kept busy selecting the best or the most significant of the books available during a given period of time . . . A reviewer does not have to be a prophet, but merely a sensitive reader who is able to perceive the quality of a new book. If the reviewer is in tune with literature, he may often make an uncanny judgment that will be justified by time.[1]

And despite the nostalgic perception of past eras as less complex or demanding than our own, the definition of a classic was as difficult to formulate nearly half a century ago as it is today. Anne T. Eaton, writing in the *New York Times Book Review* for November 12, 1933, suggested a possible touchstone:

When the question arises whether or not a new book deserves a place among the classics of children's literature that have lived for many years, as a test there is nothing better than reading it aloud. A book that seems fairly good read quickly to one's self when read aloud suddenly overwhelms us with its lack of style and substance. Reading aloud brings out the dramatic quality of a book or story. If there is humor, the sharing of it with another person doubles the fun.[2]

Not surprisingly, one of the books which most pleased her in 1933 was Margery Bianco's *The Hurdy-Gurdy Man,* for the text has the narrative flow and structure of a folk story set down fresh from the telling. It is crisp rather than coy; sentimental, perhaps, but not saccharine; refreshingly free of the dear-little-reader syndrome which, even as late as the '30s, often afflicted authors steeped in the Victorian nursery tradition. Reread today, it does not seem dated or forced.

Adding to the overall impression of excellence, in the reviewer's opinion, were the illustrations by Robert Lawson, "delightful in themselves . . . inseparably a part of the text.[3]" Later in the article she concludes

> It would be hard to find a book in which text and illustrations are more perfectly in accord. The exquisite black-and-white drawings give us the feeling that Mr. Lawson must have crossed the border into the land of Make-believe and made his pictures of scenes and people on the spot.[4]

Her comment is indicative of the uncanny judgment to which Paul Heins referred, for Lawson apparently saw in the unadorned text an opportunity to extend its meaning in a kind of visual descant, creating a full, distinctive cast of personalities. The use of varied perspectives, the inclusion of slyly caricatured portrait vignettes as well as crowd scenes, and the sense of a freer but no less careful line anticipate his later, more widely known works.

Because it represents the collaboration of two individuals whose names are still familiar, *The Hurdy-Gurdy Man* deserves more consideration than it perhaps has received in recent years. When it was first published, Margery Bianco, author of *The Velveteen Rabbit* (1922), *Poor Cecco* (1925), *The Little Wooden Doll* (1925), *The Skin Horse* (1927), and *A Street of Little Shops* (1932), to cite only five of her books, was undoubtedly a more prominent figure in the children's book field than the illustrator who would become internationally known some years later following his delineation of that archetypal but bullish flower child for Munro Leaf's *The Story of Ferdinand* (1936).

An amazingly versatile individual, English-born Margery Bianco was considered an important influence on the development of publishing for children in the United States during the 1920s and 1930s, an influence which continued until her death in 1944 at St. Vincent's Hospital, not far from her Greenwich Village home in New York City. A memorial article written for *The Horn Book Magazine* by Anne Carroll Moore in 1945 contained the following assessment of her work:

> At this time of heightened interest in the interchange of significant books with other countries, I am freshly impressed by the quality and variety of Mrs. Bianco's interests, her skill as a writer and translator, the reliability and richness of her background and, above all, by the wisdom, the humor, the spiritual integrity she brought to the field of children's books after World War I.[5]

Her most popular books, such as *The Velveteen Rabbit* and *Poor Cecco*, were inspired by family toys. Two, *The Little Wooden Doll* and *The Skin Horse* were illustrated by her daughter Pamela, a well-known artist and illustrator in her own right, and a child genius whose initial works were exhibited before she was 12. There is a sense of intimacy about these tales, designed originally, as many of them were, for the entertainment of a particular child. Yet there is a larger, more universal dimension as well, which perhaps accounts for the author's early association with such significant artists as William Nicholson for *The*

Velveteen Rabbit and Arthur Rackham for *Poor Cecco*.

In contrast, Robert Lawson, although well known as a successful illustrator, was a comparative newcomer to the children's book field. From 1914 to 1929, with a short hiatus for service in France with the 40th Engineers, Camouflage Section, A. E. F., he had served a long apprenticeship as a commercial artist, designing greeting cards, posters, and advertisements, doing magazine illustration and even, in the Greenwich Village years prior to 1918, painting an occasional portrait and designing costumes and scenery for the Washington Square Players (later the Theatre Guild). Then, in 1929, as a failing economy diminished the market for commercial art, he turned to etching, and received the John Taylor Arms Prize of the Society of American Etchers in 1931, and, in 1932, the honor of designing the annual members' plate. During these years, he also received his first commissions as an illustrator of books for children: Arthur Mason's *The Wee Men of Ballywooden* (1930), *The Roving Lobster* (1931), and *From the Horn of the Moon* (1931); Ella Young's *The Unicorn with Silver Shoes* (1932); and Barbara Ring's *Peik* (1932).

Less prominent, perhaps, than Margery

Bianco in 1933, Lawson is today the more widely known for a much more substantial body of work. To date, the only individual to win both the Caldecott and Newbery Medals, he holds a unique position in the history of American literature for children. Unlike many illustrators, he was at ease with writing and could communicate as successfully with words as with pictures. Beginning with *Ben and Me* (1939), he assumed the dual role of author-illustrator, a role in which he would continue until his death in 1957, shortly before the publication of *The Great Wheel*, a Newbery Honor Book.

But *The Hurdy-Gurdy Man*, although representative of his early period as an illustrator of children's books, is by no means a lesser example of his talent. It is pivotal in that it not only reflects the meticulous line learned as an etcher but also because it anticipates the freer interpretation of text characteristic of his later work and is a fine example of the particular artistic philosophy which he articulated in 1935:

> ... just what is meant by illustration — is it merely to do in pictures what the author has already done in words, or to go on and carry out in a pictorial and

decorative form the spirit and atmosphere the author can really only suggest? The infinite detail which it is possible to put in a drawing to enhance the scene, would, all too often, if written, hopelessly retard the action and drama of the narrative. To my mind this is the true function of the illustrator. He must steep himself in the atmosphere of the book and then transfer that feeling to his drawings.[5]

Evaluated against this statement, *The Hurdy-Gurdy Man* may be viewed as the felicitous blending of two distinct yet mutually compatible elements: a straightforward text, which emphasizes the role of the title character, and detailed, imaginative drawings, which focus on the supporting cast. Lawson's choice of perspective was an inspired one for it offered a less static subject. By delineating the effects of the music rather than the appearance of the musician, he captured and reinforced the essential theme of the story, fleshed out the various characters, and developed visually a supplementary series of comic vignettes.

The Hurdy-Gurdy Man is not a picture story book in the absolute sense; it is probably closer in conception to an illustrated story, yet the explicit drawings, narrative in spirit, are complementary additions rather than merely decorative distractions. Not as burdened with significant quotes as *The Velveteen Rabbit,* which in recent years has engendered a cult of devotees, it seems easier and more enjoyable to tell or to read aloud. It is a lighthearted assertion — in words and pictures — of the need for joy as well as purpose, for recreation as well as work.

When the hurdy-gurdy man first whistled his way into the dour little village so preoccupied with material concerns that it had forgotten the pleasures of music, laughter, and friendship, the world was suffering from the twin woes of economic depression and international disharmony. A vagrant Pan, he set the townsfolk to dancing and then, unnoticed by the revellers, simply vanished. But not perhaps forever for the author speculated that "Somewhere undoubtedly, at that moment, he was walking the road whistling, with his monkey on his shoulder, looking for another little town that might need his music" (p. 56). Or possibly, for another troubled age which sorely needs the leavening influence of humor.

Mary M. Burns
Framingham, Massachusetts

References

1. Paul Heins, "Coming to Terms with Criticism," *The Horn Book Magazine,* 46 (August, 1970), p. 373.

2. Anne T. Eaton, "This Year's Books for Children," *The New York Times Book Review,* 12 November 1933, p. 10, col. 5.

3. Eaton, p. 10, col. 5.

4. Eaton, p. 20, col. 2.

5. Anne Carroll Moore, "Margery Williams Bianco, 1881-1944," *The Horn Book Magazine,* 21 (May-June, 1945), p. 157.

6. Robert Lawson, "Lo, the Poor Illustrator," *The Publishers' Weekly,* 128 (December 7, 1935), p. 2092.

THE HURDY-GURDY MAN

IT WAS on a bright spring morning that the hurdy-gurdy man came to town. The sky was blue; there were little green leaves on the maple trees, and the sun shone down on the roofs and sidewalks, making everything look clean and newly washed. The storekeepers were just taking down their shutters and the housewives shaking rugs, and there was a pleasant early morning smell of wood smoke and coffee, which made the hurdy-gurdy man feel very hungry, for he had walked a long way since daybreak. And the first person he set eyes on, as he strode whistling into the town with his hurdy-

gurdy strapped to his back, was the fat woman in the Delicatessen Store, just sweeping off her doorstep for the day.

"Good morning! Can I get a cup of coffee here?" asked the hurdy-gurdy man.

The fat woman looked him up and down, for he was very shabby. Still, a customer was a customer, and she was just about to say "yes," when she caught sight of a queer little wrinkled face staring at her over his shoulder. It belonged to the hurdy-gurdy man's monkey, who was perched up there atop of the organ, making no sound but just gazing at her out of his dark solemn eyes.

"You may buy a cup of coffee," she said, "but you can't bring that nasty grinning monkey into my shop, for monkeys I can't and won't abide!"

"Then, in that case," said

7

the hurdy-gurdy man politely, "we will do without the coffee!"

And off he strolled up the street with his monkey on his shoulder.

Presently he came to the Bakery, and there was the Baker in his shirt-sleeves, setting out his fresh loaves on the counter.

"Good morning! Can I get a cup of coffee here and a loaf of bread?" asked the hurdy-gurdy man.

8

But the Baker too had caught sight of the monkey, staring at him with unwinking eyes.

"I can sell you bread," he answered, "but you'll get your coffee somewhere else, for I won't have that foreign-looking beast sitting at my table and scaring my customers."

"Then we won't have the bread either," said the hurdy-gurdy man, and he went on his way.

Now it so happened that the hurdy-gurdy man had come to the worst little town he could possibly have found. It was a neat and prosperous little town, but all the people who lived in it were so busy being neat and prosperous that they had no time for anything else. Everyone went about his or her business all day long just as serious as ants in an ant-hill. The housewives worked from morning till night. Every window-

9

pane was polished till it shone; every hedge was clipped, and on the front lawns there wasn't so much as a single grass-blade out of place. And as for such things as tramps or stray

dogs or organ-grinders, the little town would have none of them.

It was a neat and prosperous little town——

THE HURDY-GURDY MAN

As the hurdy-gurdy man strolled on up the street that spring morning he looked about him. He noticed the shiny window-panes and the front curtains all starched and stiff, and the neat lawns, and once in a while he frowned, and once in a while he nodded, and once in a while he reached his hand up to scratch the ear of the little monkey who sat so quietly on his shoulder. And so he went his way, whistling through his teeth, and presently he reached the end of the Green where the tall maple trees stood. And there, a little back from the road, he came upon two small cottages, side by side.

These two little cottages didn't look as if they belonged to the town at all, and that was exactly what the town itself felt about them. They were shabby and tumble-down; their walls needed painting and their front fences were unmended, and

13

their door-yards, instead of being neat and tidy like all the
other door-yards round about, were just a tangle of roses and

14

lilacs and snow-berry bush, growing any way at all that they
chose. And in one yard there were yellow day-lilies crowding

against the palings and overflowing into the street itself, and in the other a great bed of johnny-jump-ups, hollowed out in the middle where a big striped cat lay curled up asleep in the sun.

Most unsightly little cottages, the whole town agreed.

But for all that there was something gay and cheerful about them, if only for the way the lilacs nodded in the breeze, and the sturdy look of the geraniums on the window-sills. And there was something cheerful about the people who lived in them, which was more than could be said for the rest of the townsfolk, and more too than those same townsfolk could understand.

For why should Mrs. Meeks be cheerful, with a seven year old boy called Tommy to cook and wash and buy shoes for, and only an odd day's work to be had now and then at scrubbing or spring-cleaning? While as for Miss Gay, the Dress-maker next door, everyone knew she was as poor as a church mouse, and wouldn't be able to live at all if the neighbors didn't kindly give her a few curtains to hem once in a while, because, after all, she did sew more cheaply than anyone else.

MISS GAY

None of these things the hurdy-gurdy man knew, but

17

something about the cottages seemed to please him, for he walked right in through the first gateway—which happened to be Miss Gay's—and up the little path past the johnny-jump-ups and the sleeping cat, and was just about to knock at the door, when the door opened, and there stood Miss Gay herself, a little flustered, and peering short-sightedly through her glasses.

Straight past him she peered, and straight at the little brown face staring over his shoulder, and the first thing she said was:

"Why, look at the dear little monkey!"

At that the monkey moved for the first time. He scrambled down from his master's shoulder and ran through the doorway into Miss Gay's kitchen. He climbed into a chair at the

table where Miss Gay had been eating her breakfast, and
there he sat.

"See that, bless him!" Miss Gay exclaimed. "He must be
hungry! And perhaps you'd take a cup of coffee, too," she

added, turning to the hurdy-gurdy man. "It's early in the day to be travelling."

"I will indeed, thank you," said the hurdy-gurdy man, and he followed her in and sat down at the table and took the monkey on his knee.

Miss Gay asked him no questions, but she bustled about and fetched coffee and bread and home-made jam, and an apple for the monkey. When everything was on the table she said, "And now, if you'll excuse me, I must go and call Tommy Meeks next door, for he'd never forgive me if he knew I'd had a monkey to breakfast, and he wasn't here to see him."

And she fluttered out at the door calling: "Tommy! Tommy Meeks! Come and see who's here!"

Tommy was tanned and brown-haired and freckled, and

his toes, as usual, were nearly out of his shoes, but the monkey
took to him amazingly, and he to the monkey. And while

they were making friends, and the monkey offering Tommy bites of his apple, the hurdy-gurdy man asked Miss Gay what she thought about the town.

"They're nice people," Miss Gay told him. "No one could say they aren't kind. But there—they're just taken up with their own affairs. Now where I was born the folk were all neighborly, and they liked to joke or gossip, and if there was music they'd gather round from miles to hear it! But here they aren't like that. They're folk that like everything quiet.

And as for a bit of music, you couldn't get them to listen
to it!"

23

"They'll listen to my music," said the hurdy-gurdy man.

"Goodness knows they need it," Miss Gay nodded. "Though I shouldn't be talking about my neighbors this way. But I always liked to see things cheerful!"

"How many tunes can your organ play?" interrupted Tommy. He wanted to know all about it, and how the stops worked.

"It can play three tunes, but as a rule there are only two of them I ever need to play," said the hurdy-gurdy man. "If I pull out that third stop there, then it plays the third tune."

"And what is that like?" Tommy asked.

"It's a queer sort of a tune," said the hurdy-gurdy man, "and I don't play it so often."

"Oh, I hope you play it today!" Tommy cried.

"That we'll see about," said the hurdy-gurdy man. "And now, thank you very much for the break-fast, and we'll have to be getting along!"

At that the monkey swallowed his last bite of apple, very quickly, and jumped to his master's shoul-der, and the man picked up his hurdy-gurdy once more and set out.

Tommy went with him. He was very anxious to hear the music, and he didn't mean to lose sight of his friend the monkey.

25

THE HURDY-GURDY MAN

When they came to the middle of the Green the hurdy-gurdy man stopped. He unslung the strap from his shoulder and began to play. As he turned the handle the first little tune tinkled out, a funny wheezy old tune, such as all hurdy-gurdies play, with a lot of squeaks and trills and deep rumblings to it.

No one seemed to be listening. Here and there a window blind was whisked aside and then whisked back again, in an annoyed sort of way. But no one paid any real attention.

But by the time he had begun his little tune for the second time, someone had heard him certainly.

The children had heard him.

For it is a queer thing that, whatever the grown people may be like in a town, the children are the same the world

The children had heard him.

RL

over, and all children love a hurdy-gurdy. So out they came trooping, to gather round the hurdy-gurdy man and his monkey. Children just escaped from the breakfast table, boys and girls on their way to school, they all came scampering across the grass, shouting one to another and paying no heed at all to their parents, who scolded them from the doorways. All they thought of was to see the monkey and listen to the hurdy-gurdy.

When the hurdy-gurdy man played his second tune it was even better than the first. It went faster and had a gayer lilt to it, so that all the children began to prance and jump, while the monkey pulled his cap off and bobbed and ducked to them till they yelled with joy.

And now the school bell began to ring. "Ding-dong, ding-

dong," it went, but no one paid any attention to it. And after it had been ringing for a long time, and still no one obeyed it, the Teacher herself came out on the school-house steps, and began to clap her hands at the children very sternly and angrily.

But no one paid any attention to her, either.

THE HURDY-GURDY MAN

Every child in the town, by now, was gathered round the hurdy-gurdy.

Such a thing had never been heard of before!

The fathers and mothers were furious, the School Teacher was furious. The Town Clerk was the most fu-

34

rious of all for he liked quiet and order, and here, almost un-
der the very Town Hall windows, was such a hullabaloo as
he had never heard before. He wanted to fetch the police, but
he knew that the Town Policeman (there was only one) was

in bed that day with a bad cold in his head, and couldn't be

35

routed out. For when had their quiet orderly town ever expected to *need* a policeman?

Out came the Town Clerk himself, waving his hands and spluttering, his pen behind his ear.

"You must go away," he cried. "This is disgraceful! Street music isn't allowed in this town!"

But the hurdy-gurdy man went right on grinding out his tune.

"Do you hear me?" shouted the Town Clerk. "And as for you," he went on, glaring at the mob of children, "go right into school this minute, every one of you!"

But through the noise of the hurdy-gurdy his words only sounded like "Hoo—hoo—hoo!"

"Hoo—hoo!" the children shouted back at him, for they

36

were feeling too happy and excited by this time to care what anyone said to them, whether they could hear it or not.

"I shall fetch the Mayor!" stormed the Town Clerk.

And fetch the Mayor he did.

The Mayor came, puffing and blowing, with his hat on the back of his head. He had been an auctioneer before he was made Mayor, and he still had the auctioneer's manner.

"Now then," boomed the Mayor. "Now then!"

It sounded like: "Step up! Step up!"

And everyone stepped up, for by this time half the towns-folk had gathered round, too.

The Mayor pulled a copy of the town by-laws from his pocket and began to read, very fast.

"Whereas, it is hereby decreed that any person or persons causing an obstruction——"

He had just got to the word "obstruction" when the monkey jumped down from the hurdy-gurdy man's shoulder, took a flying leap onto the Mayor's broad back, snatched the copy

38

——where he sat, tearing the paper into tiny shreds.

of the by-laws out of his hand and scrambled up with it to the top of the village flagstaff, where he sat, tearing the paper into tiny shreds and dropping them down on the heads of the crowd below.

"Arrest that monkey!" shouted the Mayor. "Shoot that monkey!"

"Don't you dare!" piped a thin little voice from the out-skirts of the crowd. It belonged to Miss Gay, the Dress-maker.

"Shoot him!" shouted the townsfolk. "Shoot him!"

There was a great confusion and noise and fuss, with every-one yelling at the tops of their voices but, through it all, the hurdy-gurdy kept on its tinkling tune.

Meantime Tommy Meeks, who was far more interested in the hurdy-gurdy than in anything else, tugged suddenly at the organ-man's sleeve.

"Play the third tune!" he said. "I want to hear the third tune!"

The hurdy-gurdy man looked down at Tommy, and he looked round on the crowd.

"Yes," he said, "I think now we'll play the third tune!"

44

And he pushed in that little stop at the side of the hurdy-gurdy that Tommy had been so anxious about all the time.

All at once the hurdy-gurdy broke out into the very maddest and jiggiest little tune that has ever been heard. It was like all the tunes in the world rolled up into one, and yet it was like none of them. It was the sort of little tune that set your brain whirling and your feet jigging, whether you wanted or not.

45

THE HURDY-GURDY MAN

At the first notes the townsfolk forgot all about the monkey and the Mayor and the flagstaff. They just stood there and stared. And then a very queer and surprised look came

over all their faces. And their heads began to nod and their feet began to fidget, and before they knew it they were all dancing!

There they all were, the Town Clerk and the Druggist, the Grocer and the cross Baker, the fat woman from the Delicatessen Shop, the housewives and all the rest of them, dancing away to the music of the hurdy-gurdy; cheery Mrs. Meeks having the time of her life for once, and little Miss Gay holding up her skirts and skipping with the best of them!

"Stop it!" gasped the Mayor. "Stop it, stop it!" begged the School Teacher, her head bobbing and her spectacles bouncing on her nose. But no one could stop it, and soon they were too much out of breath even to gasp.

Round and round the Green they went, children and grown folk all together, dancing away like mad, while the hurdy-gurdy wheezed out its strange jiggety tune, and the monkey, who by now had slid down the flagstaff again and was perched

47

——they were all dancing.

on his master's shoulder, waved his little red cap and cheered
them on.

And then, suddenly, the music stopped.

Down everyone tumbled, one on top of another, too dizzy
to stand on their feet another second. The Town Clerk went
sprawling on the grass; the Delicatessen lady clutched the

Baker and over they went in a heap, and the School Teacher sat down plump on the Mayor's lap. Red-faced, panting and out of breath, there they sat and stared at one another.

And very silly they all felt!

There was only one thing to do about it. Everyone began to laugh. The others all looked so foolish that they couldn't help it. They laughed and they choked, and they held their sides and laughed again.

The Mayor was the first who could get his breath to speak. And what he said was the strangest thing of all. He said:

"Let's have a picnic!"

For that's what the music had done to *him!*

"A picnic, a picnic!" shouted all the children. "A picnic!" shouted everyone else.

The Delicatessen lady billowed to her feet.

"I'll bring the hot dogs and sandwiches!" she cried.

"I'll bring the buns!" cried the Baker.

52

"I'll fetch the ice cream and the soda!" shouted the Druggist.

And away they went.

It was the best picnic the town had ever had. In fact it was the very first picnic that the town had ever had. No one worried about anything. There was no time to run home and brush one's hair or put on one's best clothes. Everyone just sat round on the grass in a big circle, with the Mayor in the middle, and ate and drank and enjoyed themselves.

And it was not until Tommy Meeks was munching his seventh doughnut and scraping his third plate of ice cream, that he looked around and cried out suddenly: "Why, where is the hurdy-gurdy man?"

Where, indeed?

THE HURDY-GURDY MAN

The hurdy-gurdy man had vanished. No one had seen him go. He had just disappeared.

Somewhere undoubtedly, at that moment, he was walking the road whistling, with his monkey on his shoulder, looking for another little town that might need his music.

ANN A. Flowers, Patricia Lord, and Betsy Groban edited the introductory material in this book, which was phototypeset on a Mergenthaler 606-CRT typesetter in Primer and Primer Italic typefaces by Trade Composition of Springfield, MA. This book was printed and bound by Braun-Brumfield, Inc. of Ann Arbor, Michigan.

Gregg Press
Children's Literature Series
Ann A. Flowers and
Patricia Lord, *Editors*

When Jays Fly to Bárbmo by Margaret
Balderson. New Introduction by Anne Izard.

Cautionary Tales by Hilaire Belloc. New
Introduction by Sally Holmes Holtze.

The Hurdy-Gurdy Man by Margery Williams
Bianco. New Introduction by
Mary M. Burns.

Nurse Matilda by Christianna Brand. New
Introduction by Sally Holmes Holtze.

Azor and the Blue-Eyed Cow by Maude
Crowley. New Introduction by
Eunice Blake Bohanon.

The Village That Slept by Monique Peyrouton
de Ladebat. New Introduction by
Charlotte A. Gallant.

Squirrel Hotel by William Pène du Bois. New
Introduction by Paul Heins.

The Boy Jones by Patricia Gordon. New
Introduction by Lois Winkel.

The Little White Horse by Elizabeth Goudge.
New Introduction by Kate M. Flanagan.

The <u>Minnow</u> Leads to Treasure by A. Philippa Pearce. New Introduction by Ethel Heins.

The Maplin Bird by K. M. Peyton. New Introduction by Karen M. Klockner.

Ounce, Dice, Trice by Alastair Reid. New Introduction by Elizabeth Johnson.

The Sea of Gold and Other Tales from Japan by Yoshiko Uchida. New Introduction by Marcia Brown.

Dear Enemy by Jean Webster. New Introduction by Ann A. Flowers.

Mistress Masham's Repose by T. H. White. New Introduction by Ann A. Flowers.